For Susanne, with love
– R.E.
For Natasha Fenton, with love
– S.W.

Originally published in the United Kingdom in 2003 by Frances Lincoln Limited,
4 Torriano Mews, Torriano Avenue, London NW5 2RZ England
Printed in Singapore.
All rights reserved.
www.harperchildrens.com

Library of Congress Cataloging-in-Publication Data is available.

2 3 4 5 6 7 8 9 10
❖
First U.S. Edition

Good Night, Copycub

BY Richard Edwards

PICTURES BY Susan Winter

HarperCollinsPublishers

It was a busy day. Copycub and his mother spent hours playing in the woods. Copycub chased his mother. His mother chased Copycub. They dug in the ground for roots to eat. His mother found one and crunched it up. Copycub found one too.

Copycub was tired out when he lay down in the bear cave that night. But when he closed his eyes, he couldn't fall asleep.

He turned over one way, but the floor felt bumpy.

He turned over the other way, but the floor felt lumpy.

He curled up to his mother's side and got too hot.

He rolled away from his mother's side and got too cold.

And at last with all his wiggling, he woke up his mother.

She yawned. "What's the matter, Copycub?"

"I can't fall asleep."

"Do you want me to tell you a story?"

"Yes, please," Copycub said. He loved stories.

"Once upon a time," his mother began, "there was a small bear named . . ."

"Copycub!" the small bear said happily.

"That's right. And do you know why he was called Copycub? Because he was always copying."

Copycub smiled.

"One night," his mother said quietly, "Copycub couldn't fall asleep, and with all his wiggling, he woke up his mother. So they went for a walk in the moonlight.

"Copycub and his mother walked slowly down the hillside. Everything was quiet. Millions of stars sparkled in the sky, and a full moon was shining. The bears went through the woods until they came to a lake, where they saw something white floating on the water."

"What was it?" Copycub asked.

"A goose," replied his mother. "A white goose sleeping in the moonlight."

"Fast asleep?"

"Safe and sound," his mother whispered.

"When they got back to their cave, Copycub's mother asked him a question: Who's good at copying?"

"I am!" Copycub said.

"Yes, you are," his mother said, coming to the end of her story. "So when you can't fall asleep, just think of the white goose sleeping on the lake. And the moose sleeping in the shadows. And the hare fast asleep in the grass . . ."

"And copy them?"

"That's right, Copycub."

The small bear closed his eyes.
He thought of the animals outside,
all sleeping safe and sound.

   "I'll copy them," he murmured.

"Good night, goose.

Good night, moose.   Good night, hare. . . ."

"They started to walk back up the hill when they saw something curled up in the grass."

"What was it?"

"A hare," said his mother. "A brown hare sleeping under the stars."

"Fast asleep?" asked Copycub.

"Safe and sound."

"Then the two bears turned from the lake and padded softly into the forest, where they saw a big, dark shape."

"What was it?"

"A moose," replied his mother, "sleeping in the shadows."

"Fast asleep?" asked Copycub.

"Safe and sound."

Copycub yawned. "And what did the bears do then?"